THE
EASY CLASSICS
EPIC COLLECTION

Published by Sweet Cherry Publishing Limited
Unit 36, Vulcan House,
Vulcan Road,
Leicester, LE5 3EF
United Kingdom

First published in the UK in 2021
2021 edition

2 4 6 8 10 9 7 5 3 1

ISBN: 978-1-78226-784-3

© Sweet Cherry Publishing

The Easy Classics Epic Collection: Crime and Punishment

Based on the original story by Fyodor Dostoevsky,
adapted by Gemma Barder.
All rights reserved. No part of this publication may be
reproduced or utilised in any form or by any means, electronic
or mechanical, including photocopying, recording, or using
any information storage and retrieval system, without prior
permission in writing from the publisher.

The right of Gemma Barder to be identified as the author of this
work has been asserted by her in accordance with the Copyright,
Design and Patents Act 1988.

Cover design by Helen Panayi and Dominika Plocka
Illustrations by Helen Panayi

Lexile® code numerical measure L = Lexile® 670L

www.sweetcherrypublishing.com

Printed and bound in the United Kingdom
E.C007

Crime and Punishment

Fyodor Dostoevsky

Sweet Cherry

The Raskolnikovs

Mrs Raskolnikov
Head of the family

Rodya Raskolnikov
Son

Dounia Raskolnikov
Daughter

Dimitri Razumikhin
Rodya's friend

The Marmeladovs

Marmeladov
Head of the family

Sofya Marmeladov
Daughter

The Ivanovnas

Alyona Ivanovna
Elderly pawnbroker

Lizaveta Ivanovna
Sister

Officer Zamyotov
Police officer

Detective Petrovich
Detective

Pyotr Luzhin
Dounia's fiancé

Svidrigailov
Dounia's former employer

Chapter One

Rodya Raskolnikov sat on his sagging bed and looked around his tiny apartment. He lived in a poor corner of St Petersburg. Wallpaper peeled from the walls and the carpet was worn and patchy. He ran his hands through his long auburn hair. How had his life ended up like this? Once, he had been the most talented law student at his university. Now, he spent his days wondering where his next meal would come from.

If only I had money, Raskolnikov thought, wringing his hands. *If I had money, I could pay my fees, return to my studies and become a lawyer. I could help so many people.*

Raskolnikov knew someone who had plenty of money. Alyona Ivanovna was an old pawnbroker. She gave people small amounts of money for expensive items, then sold them on for a large profit.

She saw a person's desperation and used it to become rich.

Raskolnikov had been to see Alyona a few times. In desperation to pay for food and rent, he had sold many of his precious belongings to her.

She is just one life, Raskolnikov thought. *One life compared to the thousands I could help once I pay my fees and qualify as a lawyer.*

Raskolnikov was putting together a plan. He needed to turn his life around and he knew just how to do it. He would kill Alyona Ivanovna and take her money.

It was the worst thing he had ever imagined himself doing, but he felt as though he had no choice.

'Who is there?' asked a weak, trembling voice from behind the pawnbroker's shop door. Alyona Ivanovna was ancient and frail.

'It is me, Miss Ivanovna,' said Raskolnikov. 'Rodya Raskolnikov. We have met before. I have come to show you my watch. I am in need of more money.'

Slowly, Alyona Ivanovna opened the door to let Raskolnikov into the shop. She was small and hunched over with age. The shop was dark and musty. Rings, necklaces, clocks and all sorts of precious items glittered from behind dusty

glass cases. Raskolnikov noticed some of his own possessions on display.

'This is my watch,' Raskolnikov said. It was one of the last things he owned that he could sell. 'I think it is worth quite a few coins.'

The old lady turned to fetch her magnifying glass.

This is it! thought Raskolnikov. *This is my chance!*

But he could not do it. At that moment, killing someone was something he thought he would never be able to do. Instead, he accepted the coins the old lady offered him for his watch, and started to leave the shop.

Raskolnikov was angry at himself. He had been so certain of his plan and now he had lost his chance to carry it out. He shook his head in frustration.

'Actually,' he said as he stepped onto the street, 'I have a jewellery box I would like to show you as well. It's worth far more than my old watch.'

Alyona Ivanovna narrowed her eyes. 'Fine,' she said. 'Bring it to me and I will take a look.'

Chapter Two

Raskolnikov returned to his apartment feeling deflated. He had been so close to completing his plan, but he had been too weak to go through with it. He could only hope that his courage would not fail him again when he returned later with the jewellery box.

Raskolnikov spotted a letter laying on his doormat. He recognised the handwriting straight away.

Dear son,

I am writing to you with news of your sister, Dounia. As you know, these past months she has been earning good money as a nanny with the family of a man called Svidrigailov. Unfortunately, she has had to leave that job. Svidrigailov has confessed that he is in love with Dounia, despite the fact that he already has a wife. Dounia feels she must leave the home, and that terrible man, at once.

We do not have much money. What little money we had, we used to fund your studies. Without your support, Dounia has no choice but to marry so that we can survive. Pyotr Luzhin has long wished to make Dounia his wife. He is rich and respectable ...

Raskolnikov screwed up the letter and threw it across the room. From his mother's letters, Raskolnikov knew that Dounia could do far better than Pyotr Luzhin. He was rich but arrogant, and would treat Dounia little better than a maid. Raskolnikov knew that marrying him was the last thing Dounia would want. But she had been forced into accepting Luzhin's proposal because of Raskolnikov's studies and dreams.

Raskolnikov stood up, determined. It was almost as though someone else, someone far stronger, had invaded his body. This time, he would not back out of his plan. His mother's letter was more proof that it was the only path he could take. He must take Alyona Ivanovna's money to not only become a lawyer, but to save his sister from having to marry such a man.

Raskolnikov slipped out of his apartment and took an axe from the woodshed in the alley, hiding it inside his coat. He headed back to the pawnbroker's shop.

Chapter Three

Raskolnikov woke up in a daze. He was on the sofa where he had collapsed with exhaustion the previous night. His mind raced with what he had done. He had killed Alyona Ivanovna and pocketed her money and handfuls of jewels. His plan was complete – but it had not gone as expected.

The pawnbroker's sister, Lizaveta, had arrived at the shop. Because she had seen what he had done, Raskolnikov felt he had no choice but to kill her as well. Raskolnikov had not wanted to kill Lizaveta, but it could not be helped. Besides, he would use the money to pay for his studies, and what were two lives in payment for the thousands he could help when he became a qualified lawyer?

Raskolnikov was deep in these desperate thoughts when the door to his apartment rattled with a knock. He peered around the door to see an important-looking envelope on his doormat, bearing the official crest of the St Petersburg Police. Certain that the police had discovered what he had done, Raskolnikov opened the envelope with trembling hands. The letter contained an official request for him to go to the police station that morning.

'You are Rodya Raskolnikov?' asked the young police officer. Raskolnikov nodded, unable to speak. 'Thank you for coming in, Mr Raskolnikov. My name is Officer Zamyotov. We have had a complaint about you, I'm afraid.'

Raskolnikov's throat was dry. 'A complaint?' he croaked.

'Yes, from your landlady. She says you haven't paid your rent for nearly three months.' Officer Zamyotov scratched his head and

shuffled some papers in front of him. 'Is this true?'

Filled with relief, Raskolnikov found his voice. 'I am afraid so, Officer. I find myself a little down on my luck at the moment.'

Officer Zamyotov shook his head. 'I understand,' he said, kindly. 'There are a lot of people in the same situation. Some people are so desperate they end up doing terrible things.'

Raskolnikov looked up. 'What sort of things?' he asked.

'Just this morning, the old pawnbroker and her sister were

found dead in her shop. Someone had killed them for money and a handful of jewels,' replied Officer Zamyotov.

Raskolnikov's head began to swim. 'How … how awful,' he said. 'Do they know who might have done it?'

Officer Zamyotov stared at Raskolnikov for a moment before answering. 'Not yet, but it is only a matter of time. People who commit these types of crimes are always found out in the end.'

Raskolnikov did not hear anything else. He fell to the ground and the world went black.

Chapter Four

Raskolnikov opened his eyes and remembered where he was.

'Are you okay, Mr Raskolnikov?' Officer Zamyotov asked, handing Raskolnikov a glass of water. 'I'm afraid you fainted.'

'I am fine,' Raskolnikov lied. He needed to get away from the police station. 'I haven't eaten today, that is all.'

Officer Zamyotov nodded. 'It seemed as though the news of the murders upset you,' he observed. 'Did you know Miss Ivanovna?'

'No,' Raskolnikov said quickly. 'I mean, yes, a little. She bought my watch from me just yesterday. But we weren't friends.'

Officer Zamyotov stared at Raskolnikov as the glass in his hand began to shake.

'Thank you for your help,' said Raskolnikov, carefully standing.

'I will be sure to pay my landlady as soon as I can.'

Without waiting for the officer's response, Raskolnikov stepped out of the police station into the cool air of the day. He felt light-headed and shaken. He decided to call on one of his old friends who lived at the university close by, where they had both spent many happy days.

Dimitri Razumikhin was the same age as Raskolnikov, but he looked ten years younger. His hair was short and neat and he wore smart clothes. He was strong and healthy, as Raskolnikov had once been. His apartment at the university was clean, warm and tidy.

Dimitri was pleased to welcome his old friend inside, but he was concerned about Raskolnikov's appearance. He looked thin, sickly and tired.

'Why not stay with me for a few days?' said Dimitri. 'I have plenty of room.'

Raskolnikov shook his head. 'I am fine. I just wanted to see a friendly face. Hopefully it will not be long before I am back here at the university with you. But now I must go. I am feeling quite tired.'

'At least let me walk you home,' Dimitri said.

Raskolnikov leant on his friend's arm as they walked away from the university to a far more unpleasant side of town. Dimitri helped Raskolnikov climb the stairs to his apartment and watched as he fell onto his bed and slept.

Chapter Five

Days passed as Raskolnikov lay in bed. Dimitri tried to feed his friend, but Raskolnikov was too feverish to eat. By the fourth day, Raskolnikov began to breathe more easily. He sat up in bed and looked around him.

'What happened to me?' he asked. He wondered how much of what he thought had happened in the past few days was a dream.

'You were ill, my friend,' replied Dimitri. 'You came to see me at the university, remember?'

The reality of the past week hit Raskolnikov like a punch in the stomach. It wasn't a dream. He was a murderer. He had stolen money and jewels. And they were in the apartment! Raskolnikov could not risk Dimitri discovering them.

'I thank you for everything you have done for me,' Raskolnikov began, hurriedly. He swung his legs out of bed and got dressed. 'You must be missing a lecture. Perhaps it is time for you to leave …?'

Dimitri stood up, confused at his friend's abruptness. 'Well, of course, if you are sure?'

Before Raskolnikov could answer him, another gentleman appeared at the apartment door. The small, well-dressed man knocked, but did not wait to be asked in. He took a few steps into the apartment and looked around.

His eyes lingered on the tatty curtains and peeling wallpaper as though they were something deeply unpleasant.

'Can I help you?' Raskolnikov asked, annoyed at the intrusion.

'My name is Luzhin,' replied

the man. 'I was told the brother of my fiancée lives here, but I think I must have the wrong address.'

He looked from Raskolnikov's shabby clothes up to his messy hair.

'You do not have the wrong address, sir. I am Raskolnikov, Dounia's brother.'

Luzhin gave a little laugh. 'Well, Dounia said her family was not well off, but she didn't mention her brother was a beggar!'

At this, Dimitri stood in front of the man. His face

was stern. 'I think perhaps you should leave, sir,' Dimitri said.

'Thank you, Dimitri,' said Raskolnikov. 'I need to rest. If you could show Mr Luzhin the way downstairs, I would be most grateful. I will come and see you soon.'

Dimitri and Luzhin looked at each other, then silently left Raskolnikov's home.

Chapter Six

Raskolnikov felt the weight of his guilt on his shoulders. He now had the money to study again, but he was too scared to touch the coins and jewels he had hidden in the walls of his apartment.

Raskolnikov took a few of the coins he had received in exchange for his watch and knocked on the door of his landlady's apartment.

'How d'you get this?' the wrinkled old landlady said, counting the coins in her hand before pocketing them.

'I pawned my watch,' Raskolnikov said quietly.

'You were lucky to get to the pawnbroker before she was killed! Horrible thing.' The landlady shook her head and pulled her headscarf closer under her chin. 'Well, at least they've found the person who did it,' she sighed.

All the hairs on Raskolnikov's neck stood on end. 'They have?' he croaked.

'Some fella confessed this morning,' sniffed the landlady. 'So we can all feel safe in our beds again!'

Raskolnikov nodded and turned away. His mind swam as his feet took him out onto the street. *Someone has confessed,* he thought. *I am free.* But this knowledge did not feel as good as he thought it might. Before he realised what he was doing, Raskolnikov was standing in front of the pawnbroker's shop. Police officers surrounded it.

'Good morning, Mr Raskolnikov,' said a familiar voice. It was Officer Zamyotov. 'You are looking better.'

Raskolnikov tried to smile. 'Thank you. I hear someone has confessed to the murders,' he said.

'Yes,' replied the officer, cheerfully. 'Case closed, it seems.'

'It is far from closed,' came the voice of an older gentleman. Officer Zamyotov introduced him as Porfiry Petrovich, a senior detective in charge of the murder case.

'Why do you say that?' Raskolnikov asked, avoiding the detective's gaze.

'Because hardly anyone

who commits a murder admits to it. And this man was seen elsewhere in town at the time the murders took place. It was not him,' Detective Petrovich replied.

Raskolnikov's heart was beating hard in his chest. 'Why would someone admit to murder when they are innocent?'

Detective Petrovich stared at Raskolnikov, who kept his eyes firmly on the pawnbroker's shop. 'People do strange things, Mr Raskolnikov,' he said. 'It is our job to bring them to justice.'

Chapter Seven

Raskolnikov did not like the detective. He felt as though Detective Petrovich could see inside his mind. Raskolnikov's footsteps took him, as they often did, to an old tavern. It was a place where none of his old university friends would go. He could drink there without having to explain how far he had fallen from his old life.

As he approached the tavern, he saw a commotion outside. An old man had been trapped under a carriage. Raskolnikov recognised Marmeladov immediately, as the two men had spoken many times inside the tavern. Marmeladov would often warn Raskolnikov not

to end up like him, penniless and relying on his daughter to bring home whatever money she could.

'Stand aside!' said Raskolnikov. 'I know this man.'

'There's nothing that can be done for him!' said the carriage driver. 'He came out of nowhere!'

Marmeladov was badly hurt. Raskolnikov could hear him trying to speak, and he knelt beside the old man. 'Take me home to Sofya, Rodya,' Marmeladov whispered.

With all the strength he could summon, Raskolnikov heaved the old man onto his feet. And with one arm around his shoulders, he took him home.

The door to Marmeladov's tiny house was opened by a young woman. She was tall and thin, and had Marmeladov's dark eyes. Her name was Sofya.

'Papa!' she cried. Together,

they helped Marmeladov to a worn sofa.

Sofya held her father. 'You need to see a doctor,' she told him.

'I don't think anything can be done to help,' Raskolnikov said quietly.

'Are you a doctor?' the young woman asked Raskolnikov, pleadingly.

'No, I study the law,' he answered. Then, he added quietly, 'But I do know when a person is beyond hope.'

Sofya buried her face in her father's coat as he closed his eyes. After a few moments, his breathing stopped, and Marmeladov was gone.

Raskolnikov stayed with Sofya for a little while afterwards. He explained how he and Marmeladov were friends.

'He wanted to come home before he died. He wanted to be with you,' said Raskolnikov. 'He talked of you often.'

Sofya nodded and wiped her tears. 'I do not know what I will do without him,' she replied. 'And I have no money to pay for a funeral.'

Raskolnikov felt in his pocket for the final few coins he had left from selling his watch. He handed them to Sofya. 'Take this,' he said. 'It is not much, but it will pay for a small burial service.' He knew there was no way to bring back Sofya's father, but at least he could help her with something.

Chapter Eight

The next morning, light shone through the thin curtains as Raskolnikov rose from his bed. He thought about Marmeladov. Since he had left the university, he had few friends, but Marmeladov had been one of them. Then Raskolnikov began to think about Alyona Ivanovna.

What friends had she left behind when he had taken her life?

The night at the pawnbroker's shop felt like a dream, as though it had happened to someone else. Yesterday, Raskolnikov had been able to help Sofya in her time of need. *Surely that shows I am a good person?* Raskolnikov thought as he washed and dressed. *I must work hard to show that these crimes were not for nothing. I will help thousands of people.*

He decided to go to Dimitri's apartment. He hoped that his friend would help him enrol back in the university now that he had money for the fees.

'I am glad to see you,' Dimitri said, as he opened the door to see Raskolnikov standing there. 'But, my friend, you still look so pale.'

'I am quite well,' replied Raskolnikov. 'In fact, I want to come back to the university. I have so many plans, Dimitri, but I need your help.'

'We can talk all about that soon, but for now you need to go home and rest. Let me come with you,' Dimitri said, placing one of his scarves around Raskolnikov's neck.

Raskolnikov was still telling Dimitri of his thoughts for the future, when he opened the door to his apartment and saw his mother and Dounia sitting at the small table by the unlit fire.

'Rodya,' said his mother, getting up to greet him.

Raskolnikov was stunned. He did not know his mother and sister were planning on travelling from the small town where Dounia and Raskolnikov had grown up

to visit him. 'What are you doing here?' Raskolnikov asked, falling heavily onto the sofa.

'Your landlady let us in, brother,' Dounia said, looking from him to Dimitri.

Suddenly, Raskolnikov remembered Dimitri standing in the doorway. 'This is my friend, Dimitri Razumikhin,' he said. 'We were at university together, before ...' Raskolnikov's voice trailed off.

'Perhaps I should go?' said Dimitri.

'Oh no, do stay,' said Dounia, rising from the table. 'We might need the support of a friend to help us talk my brother round. I am afraid he will not like what we have come to say.'

Raskolnikov sat up straight as his mother explained the reason for their visit.

Chapter Nine

Raskolnikov was angry. He paced the length of his small living area as his mother spoke.

'The wedding will be in the summer,' she said. 'Luzhin has it all arranged. He has paid for everything.'

'I know you do not want to marry him, Dounia,' Raskolnikov said. 'I met him. He barged his way in here. He seems like a horrible man.'

Dounia sighed. She glanced at Dimitri who had fetched a glass of water for his friend. 'It is true. He is not the sort of man I dreamt of marrying,' she said. 'But without Luzhin's money, Mother and I will be penniless.'

Raskolnikov put his head in his hands. It was all his fault. 'Please just wait until I have finished my studies. I will get a good job and send you the money,' he said.

'You know we cannot wait that long,' his mother said, quietly.

Raskolnikov sighed. He knew it would be another year at least until he was ready to get a job in a law firm or as a clerk. And he could not hand over the money he had stolen, as they were sure to question where it had come from.

'What do you want me to do?' he asked, wearily.

Dounia smiled. 'Get better. Smarten yourself up. Show Luzhin you are as kind and caring as I know you to be,' she said. The words 'kind' and 'caring' struck Raskolnikov like two tiny knives in his heart. He knew he was neither.

'Where are you staying?' asked Raskolnikov. He suddenly longed to be alone. When he was alone, he did not have to pretend to be the person people thought he was.

'We do not have money for a hotel,' said his mother, glancing around the small apartment. 'We thought we might be able to stay with you for a few days.'

A panicked look crossed Raskolnikov's face. He could not imagine his mother sleeping in his broken bed, or his sister on the dirty floor next to her. Besides, the stolen money and jewels were still hidden in the apartment. It was impossible for them to stay with him.

'Perhaps I can help?' asked Dimitri. 'There are empty

apartments at the university for students' visitors. You can be my guests.'

Raskolnikov was more grateful to his friend than ever before. A choking pain settled in his chest as he looked from the face of his mother to his sister to his best friend. These people were so much better than him. He didn't deserve them.

Chapter Ten

The following morning, Raskolnikov got up early. He moved the stolen items out of his apartment, dug a small hole by the woodshed and hid them under the frozen ground.

When he returned, he did what he could to make his rooms

look better. He swept the floor and cleared the dirty dishes. He made his bed and opened the curtains. Raskolnikov knew that his mother and sister would return soon, and he wanted to try to be a better man for them.

'We have had a note from Luzhin,' said his mother when they arrived. She glanced around her son's small living room for somewhere to sit. Dounia guided her mother to the sofa before taking the note out of her purse.

'It says he does not want you at the wedding,' Dounia said, quietly.

Raskolnikov laughed. 'Is that so?' he said. 'Then I do not give you permission to marry him!'

Dounia shook her head. 'If you do not, you are condemning Mother and I. We will be homeless.'

Raskolnikov was full of bitter rage. That small, unpleasant man was forcing his beloved sister to marry him, and now he was trying to exclude Raskolnikov from her life.

Before he could say anything else, the family heard a gentle knocking on Raskolnikov's door. Slowly, a young woman peered into the apartment. It was Marmeladov's daughter, Sofya.

'I am sorry to disturb you,' she said, looking from Raskolnikov's face to his mother and sister. 'I did not know you had guests.'

Raskolnikov could not help feeling pleased to see her. He had thought of her many times since the awful day outside the tavern. 'Not at all. Please come in, Sofya,' he said. 'What can I do for you?'

'I wanted to invite you to my father's funeral,' Sofya said quietly. 'To say thank you for all your help.'

'Thank you,' Raskolnikov said, guiding Sofya back through the front door. 'I would be an honoured to attend the funeral.'

Sofya smiled shyly at Raskolnikov's family, and disappeared back through the door.

A silence settled in the apartment. Then Dounia spoke. 'I want you to meet with Luzhin,' she said to her brother. 'If you are capable of helping that young woman, then you can help me too. I want you at my wedding, Rodya.'

Raskolnikov nodded, feeling defeated. 'All right,' he sighed. 'I will come, but only if we meet at Dimitri's apartment. I would like to have at least one person on my side.'

Dounia agreed. If anyone could keep a meeting between her brother and her fiancé calm it was Dimitri. She had only known him for a short while, but it was clear Dimitri was a kind, thoughtful and good man. The sort of man Dounia wished she was marrying instead.

Chapter Eleven

The next morning, Raskolnikov waited on the corner outside the university building where Dimitri was attending a lecture. It was freezing cold, and Raskolnikov had not eaten. He could not touch the money he had stolen, for fear of anyone connecting it to the pawnbroker's shop. He had given the rest of his own money to Sofya on the day her father had died.

'Dimitri!' Raskolnikov called as he saw his friend emerge from the warm glow of the lecture hall.

'How long have you been waiting here?' asked Dimitri, concerned. 'Is everything well?'

'You have been so good to me and my family,' said Raskolnikov. 'But I am afraid I need another favour.'

The two friends walked together towards Dimitri's apartment. Raskolnikov explained the meeting that would take place the next day.

'Of course you may use my apartment,' said Dimitri. The one time he had met Luzhin, he had instantly disliked him. The idea that this man was to marry Dounia made him deeply unhappy. He had grown to like Dounia greatly over the past couple of days they had spent together.

Raskolnikov placed a hand on his friend's shoulder and smiled gratefully.

'Rodya Raskolnikov?' came a voice that filled Raskolnikov with fear. 'I have been hoping to run into you.'

Raskolnikov turned to see Detective Petrovich. Despite his small stature, the detective had a strong presence. He was squat, almost like a bulldog.

'Good morning, Detective,' Raskolnikov said as calmly as he could. 'This is my friend Dimitri Razumikhin. How can I help you?'

Detective Petrovich ignored Dimitri's outstretched hand. 'Mr Raskolnikov, I have been reading some of your work. You were a promising student, I believe.'

Raskolnikov smiled, but inside he was confused and fearful. Why was the detective reading his old university essays?

'I was particularly interested in an essay you wrote about certain people being *above the law*,' he said. 'Could you explain what you meant?'

Raskolnikov's heart began to thump hard against his chest. A cold sweat trickled down his back.

'I simply discussed the idea that if breaking the law meant doing more good than harm, then perhaps it should be allowed.'

Detective Petrovich nodded. 'I see,' he said.

'It was only an essay, Detective,' said Dimitri, with a small laugh. 'We have to write about all sorts of things when we study the law. It does not mean anything.'

Detective Petrovich nodded. 'I would like to discuss your thoughts further, Raskolnikov,' he said. 'Come to the station tomorrow.' He tipped his hat and walked away.

Chapter Twelve

That evening, Raskolnikov sat at a small table in the tavern, his thoughts racing. He was certain that Detective Petrovich suspected him of committing the murders.

Suddenly, Raskolnikov's thoughts were interrupted when he saw a large, well-dressed man sitting at the next table. The man was staring at him.

'Mr Raskolnikov, I would like to speak to you,' he said.

'How do you know my name?' Raskolnikov replied, scared that this man might be another detective keen to question him.

'I asked around. Someone told me you often come here. My name is Svidrigailov,' he replied, leaving his table and joining Raskolnikov's. 'I know your sister.'

At once, Raskolnikov realised who this man was. He was the married man who had employed Dounia as a nanny for his children, before she was forced to leave to get away from his romantic attentions.

'I know very well who you are, sir,'

Raskolnikov replied, trying to keep calm. 'What do you want from me?'

Svidrigailov smiled. 'Nothing. In fact, I want to give something to you,' he said.

Svidrigailov began to explain that his wife had recently passed away, leaving some money to Dounia in her will. The two women had cared for each other greatly.

'I want to give Dounia twice as much as my wife left her,' said Svidrigailov. After a pause, he added, 'If she agrees to marry me.'

Svidrigailov wrote the two amounts of money on a piece

of paper and showed them to Raskolnikov. They came to an extraordinary sum. Raskolnikov knew that Dounia would not accept the money from Svidrigailov – the very thought of him made her skin crawl. But the money from his wife would be enough to lift Dounia and their mother out of poverty, to buy a new house and keep them comfortable, at least until Raskolnikov could help them again.

And it was enough money to stop Dounia having to marry Luzhin.

'I will pass on the message, sir,' Raskolnikov said, standing. He was keen to be away from Svidrigailov. 'Will you be staying in St Petersburg?'

'I am staying at The Grand Hotel. I will stay as long as it takes for Dounia to agree to be my wife,' replied Svidrigailov.

Chapter Thirteen

The following day held no joy for Raskolnikov. In the morning, he was due to meet his family and Luzhin at Dimitri's apartment to discuss the wedding. In the afternoon, he had been summoned to the police station to talk to Detective Petrovich.

Raskolnikov wished he could disappear.

As he opened the door to Dimitri's apartment, Raskolnikov found Dounia and his mother seated on the sofa in front of a roaring fire. Luzhin was

leaning against the mantlepiece looking impatient.

'Let's get this over with,' said Luzhin to Raskolnikov. 'I do not want someone like you at my wedding, but Dounia insists.'

Raskolnikov stared at Luzhin with disgust. Then he turned to his sister. 'Dounia, Mr Svidrigailov found me yesterday to tell me that his wife has passed away. She has left you some money in her will. Enough for you not to have to marry this ridiculous man.'

'Now see here!' Luzhin began, but when Dounia stood up he fell silent.

'Is it true, Rodya?' she asked.

Raskolnikov nodded. 'He also wants to give you more money himself on the condition that you marry him. Although I think I know you well enough to guess what your response will be to that.'

Luzhin's eyes sparkled greedily. 'How much money did the wife leave her?' he asked. 'When we are married, I will be in charge of all of our money, of course.'

Raskolnikov took a step towards Luzhin with anger in his eyes. Dimitri pulled Raskolnikov away, as Dounia turned to face Luzhin.

'Mr Luzhin,' Dounia said, taking a deep breath. 'I think you know that I am not in love with you. I needed you to look after my mother and I, but now that is not necessary.' Luzhin's eyes widened as Dounia continued, 'I release you from our engagement.'

'You cannot do this!' Luzhin shouted, raising his hand as though to strike Dounia.

Dimitri rushed forward and

stood between them. 'Actually, sir, she can,' he said. 'I may only be a student of the law, but if a lady changes her mind about an engagement, she is within her rights to end it.'

Dounia handed over the engagement ring Luzhin had given her and watched as he slammed the door of Dimitri's apartment behind him.

'Well, good riddance!' clapped Dounia's mother. Dimitri and Dounia hugged happily while Raskolnikov looked on. He was happy for his sister and pleased that Luzhin was gone, but he could not feel the joy they felt. His heart was still heavy with the crimes he had committed. Raskolnikov thought he may never be happy again – and perhaps he did not deserve to be.

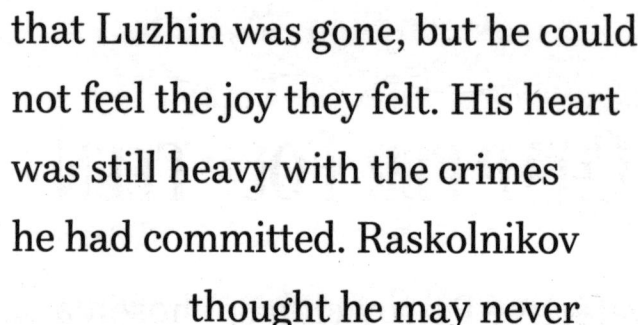

Chapter Fourteen

Detective Petrovich had chosen a small, cold, windowless room in which to talk to Raskolnikov. He placed a glass of water in front of him.

'Thank you for meeting with me,' Detective Petrovich said with a wide smile. 'I would like to ask you some questions, as you seem like a clever man. You saw Miss Ivanovna on the day she was murdered, is that correct?' he asked.

Raskolnikov nodded.

'Did you go back again after the shop was closed?'

'No,' replied Raskolnikov. 'I was at home all evening.'

'Why did you come to the police station the following day?' asked Detective Petrovich.

Raskolnikov explained that his landlady had made a complaint about his unpaid rent. He said that he hadn't eaten that day and felt ill, and so he fainted.

'And why did you come to the pawnbroker's shop the day we met?' asked Detective Petrovich.

Raskolnikov's eyes darted from side to side, searching for an answer. In truth, he did not know why.

'I was curious,' he replied.

Detective Petrovich leant closer over the table. His voice was quiet but steady. 'Mr Raskolnikov, I believe you murdered Miss Ivanovna and her sister. You had a motive to get your possessions back, and whatever else you could steal. You came to visit the scene of the crime, perhaps because you had heard that someone else had confessed. And you wrote an essay on why breaking the law is a good thing if you do it for the right reasons.'

Raskolnikov was speechless. He was too frightened to speak. Detective Petrovich was correct about everything.

Detective Petrovich leant back in his chair and spoke cheerfully. 'Of course, I have no proof, so you are free to go. But it is only a matter of time. I know you killed those women. And I will prove it.'

Chapter Fifteen

Marmeladov's funeral was held at a small church a couple of agonising days after Raskolnikov's meeting with Detective Petrovich. Sofya sat in the front row in her best hat. Raskolnikov sat as close to the door as possible. He felt uncomfortable in the house of God, remembering his terrible sins. But Raskolnikov wanted to be there to remember his friend, and to support Sofya.

After the funeral, Sofya invited the guests to the tavern. She did not have the money to offer anyone a drink or something to eat, but a small group of people went anyway. Soon, she spotted Raskolnikov sitting alone in a quiet corner, looking sickly and pale.

Raskolnikov was thinking about Detective Petrovich. He imagined being trapped in that small, windowless room where the detective had made his accusation.

'Thank you for coming,' Sofya said, sitting next to Raskolnikov. She placed her hand over his and Raskolnikov held on to it. 'Are you all right?'

'Never mind about me,' Raskolnikov said. 'How are you? Have you thought what you will do next?'

Sofya looked down. 'I do not know,' she said. 'I still have a little of the money you gave me. That will do for now.'

Suddenly, Raskolnikov was gripped with an idea. 'I have money!' he said.

'A lot of it. I cannot use it, but you can!'

Sofya shook her head. 'Forgive me, Rodya,' she said. 'But you do not look like you have money to spare.'

But it was all clear to Raskolnikov. He knew now that he could not spend the money on his university fees; Detective Petrovich was sure to ask him how he got it. But if Sofya took the stolen money to help herself and her family, then some good might come from the murders he committed.

'Sofya, please,' said Raskolnikov. 'If I give you this money that I have, you will be helping me, too.'

'I don't understand,' said Sofya. 'How will giving me money help you? Where has this money come from?'

Raskolnikov looked at the table. He had a decision to make. He could keep lying and pretend that the money came from somewhere else, or he could confess. It was terrifying, but perhaps telling someone was the right thing to do.

'The money came from Alyona Ivanovna,' he whispered at last.

Saying her name out loud made him feel sick to his stomach.

Sofya let go of Raskolnikov's hand. 'The pawnbroker who was killed?' she asked. 'And her sister?'

Raskolnikov nodded. 'I killed them. I did it to get the money for my university fees. I wanted to become a lawyer and save my sister from a horrible marriage. Now my sister has money of her own. She does not need my help. And I cannot use the money to study in case someone discovers where it came from. My wicked deed will have been for nothing unless you take the money I stole and use it yourself.'

Sofya did not say anything for a few minutes. Raskolnikov was certain she despised him. But then Sofya placed her head on Raskolnikov's shoulder and squeezed his arm. 'You have done a

great wrong,' she said at last. 'I can see that you know that. But giving me the money will not give you redemption. It will not make you feel better.'

Raskolnikov eyes filled with tears. 'Do you hate me now you know I am a murderer?' he asked.

Sofya reached into her pocket and pulled out a small wooden cross on a thin chain. She was wearing one just like it. Silently she put the necklace over Raskolnikov's head.

'I do not hate you. I know you can be a good man. You must confess to your crimes,' she said.

'And when you do, this cross will let you know that I am with you.'

Sofya kissed Raskolnikov on the forehead and left him alone. Raskolnikov was so deep in thought that he did not notice the large man watching him from the shadows. It was Svidrigailov, and he had heard everything.

Chapter Sixteen

Raskolnikov knew that it would not be long before everyone found out about his crimes. Either he would confess, or Detective Petrovich would get the evidence he needed and arrest him anyway. One way or another, he would be going to jail.

A couple of weeks ago, Raskolnikov had his future ahead of him. He had believed that by getting money, all his problems would be over. He would graduate from law school and become a celebrated lawyer. He would take on cases that helped people. He would pay back his debt to the world. But that would not happen now. Sofya had helped him realise that confession was the only way forward.

Before Raskolnikov could go to the police, he had to make sure his mother, sister and Sofya would be all right. Now Dounia had some money she could buy a small house. He was sure Dimitri would look out for them, too. In fact, he was convinced his friend was already growing quite attached to his sister.

Dounia, however, was not currently with Dimitri. She was standing outside the door to Svidrigailov's hotel room, holding a crumpled note in her trembling hands.

Dearest Dounia,

Meet me this afternoon at The Grand Hotel. I will give you the money my wife left you when she passed away. Come alone, for I have something to tell you of great importance. If you bring anyone with you, you and your whole family will be sorry.

Yours always,
Svidrigailov

'You are here!' said Svidrigailov, moving aside to let Dounia into his room. 'It is so good to see you.'

Dounia took in a deep breath as she stepped through the doorway.

'I am glad you came. I wanted to apologise for my behaviour when my wife was alive.' Svidrigailov waited for Dounia's reaction, but when she said nothing, he took a sliver of paper from his desk. 'Here is the money my wife left you. She considered you a true friend.'

Dounia gave a small nod. She took the cheque, put it in her purse and headed for the door.

'Not so fast, if you please,' said Svidrigailov. 'I have a deal to offer you.'

'You have nothing to offer me,' Dounia said. 'I don't want anything from you.'

Svidrigailov smiled, wickedly. 'Did you know your brother is a murderer?' he said. He watched with satisfaction as Dounia's face crumpled.

'That isn't true.' Her brother had fallen on hard times, and he had been acting strangely this past week, but Dounia could not believe he was capable of murder.

'I heard him myself, telling some young woman in a tavern. He said he killed the old pawnbroker and her sister to pay for his university fees. Now tell me, why would I come up with such a tale if it wasn't true?'

Dounia searched her thoughts. Her brother had changed recently. He was distracted. He became cross easily. Could he have committed these crimes?

'Now, I am willing to forget what I heard, on one condition,' Svidrigailov said.

Dounia felt sick, fearing what he was going to say next. 'Marry me, and I won't tell the police what I know.'

Dounia took a step back towards the door. She had just freed herself from one forced engagement and now she was staring at another. This time, she would be engaged to a far worse man. Luzhin was cold and a snob, but at least he did not threaten her. She had started the day with dreams of a little home with her mother. Of perhaps seeing more of Dimitri. Now, everything was crumbling around her.

Just then, Dounia spotted Svidrigailov's letter opener on the table by the door. She grabbed it and ran towards him. Svidrigailov swerved out of the way just in time. Dounia dropped the blade and began to cry.

Svidrigailov stared at Dounia. He had wanted nothing more than to be with her, no matter what it took. But she was willing to hurt him rather than marry him!

Svidrigailov sighed heavily. 'Do you hate me that much, Dounia?' he said. 'All I have done is love you.'

'You do not love!' cried Dounia.

'You bully and threaten to get what you want. You are a monster!'

Svidrigailov leant against the wall of his hotel room. He realised that he would never have Dounia's love.

'Just leave,' he said, wearily. 'I won't say anything about your wretched brother. Just go.'

Dounia ran to the door and out of the hotel to the cold streets. She did not stop running until she had reached Dimitri's apartment. As he opened the door, she fell into his arms.

Chapter Seventeen

Raskolnikov saw Svidrigailov from a distance. He had been wandering the streets of St Petersburg for half an hour, hoping that the fresh air would help him think clearly about what he was about to do. Svidrigailov was sitting on a bench with his head in his hands. Despite hating the man, Raskolnikov felt drawn to speak to him.

'What are you doing here, Svidrigailov?' he asked.

Svidrigailov looked up. His eyes were red and his face was tear-stained. 'I do not know,' he replied. 'What does it matter?'

'Have you given my sister what she is owed?' Raskolnikov asked.

Svidrigailov nodded.

Raskolnikov was about to turn and leave when Svidrigailov said: 'Who was that girl you were talking to in the tavern the other evening?'

Raskolnikov's blood ran cold. Immediately, his hand

reached for the cross around his neck. 'Sofya,' he replied. 'No one you need concern yourself with.'

Svidrigailov reached into the inside pocket of his coat and handed Raskolnikov a cheque for a huge amount of money. 'Give this to her,' he said.

Raskolnikov looked at the cheque in disbelief. 'Why?' he asked.

'It was the money I wanted to give your sister. I had hoped it would be a wedding present. But no amount of money could persuade her to love me,' Svidrigailov said. 'This girl, Sofya, seemed to have nothing. I do not need the money.' Then Svidrigailov's face changed from pity to a bitter smile. 'Perhaps she can use it to visit you in jail,' he said.

Raskolnikov's eyes shot up to meet Svidrigailov's. 'What did you say?' he hissed.

But Svidrigailov had already begun to walk away. Raskolnikov did not know where he was going, and he did not ask. All he knew was that another person now knew he murdered the pawnbroker and her sister. His time was running out. He needed to confess to the murders now, before someone else did it for him.

Chapter Eighteen

Raskolnikov stood outside Dimitri's apartment door. He could hear his mother and sister talking softly inside. Dounia was now free of Luzhin and Svidrigailov. She had money to look after their mother. And Raskolnikov was certain Dimitri was in love with his sister. The way he looked at her and took care of her was more than just friendship. Raskolnikov knew they would be happy together.

Sofya had nearly fainted when Raskolnikov handed her the money from Svidrigailov. At first, she was hesitant to take it. It seemed too good to be true. But after Raskolnikov's encouragement, she accepted it. The money would save her and her family, and perhaps she could do some good with it. Good that Raskolnikov would never get the chance to do now.

As Raskolnikov walked to the police station to confess his crimes, he took deep breaths of air and tried to remember every detail of the world around him.

The towering buildings, the sun shining through the tree branches, the way the snow piled up at the side of the road. This would be the last time he would see them as a free man.

Then, he stopped. He suddenly did not know whether he could go

through with his confession. Perhaps there was still time to fetch the stolen jewels and begin his studies again?

But as he looked around him, he saw a small figure in the distance. It was Sofya. As suddenly as he had doubted himself, Raskolnikov now knew what he had to do. He must prove himself to be a changed man to Sofya, and to his family.

On the steps of the police station, Sofya caught up with him. 'I will stand by you,' she said, taking his hand.

Raskolnikov took one last deep breath, and walked inside.

'I would like to talk to Detective Petrovich, please,' he said.

The detective walked slowly from the back of the station. He wore a small smile on his face. 'You have something to tell me?' he asked.

'Yes,' replied Raskolnikov. 'I confess to the murders of Alyona Ivanovna and her sister.'

EPILOGUE

Dimitri and Dounia were married, and Dimitri finished his studies. The happy couple lived in a smart townhouse in St Petersburg, along with Dounia's mother. When Raskolnikov was sent to prison, it broke his mother's heart. She always felt sad for the son she had lost, and what he could have been.

Sofya used her money to help what was left of her family in St Petersburg. She moved to Siberia, to a small town in the shadow of the large prison where Raskolnikov was being held for his crimes. She visited him as often as she could.

Over his years in prison, Raskolnikov understood the seriousness of his crimes. He could no longer fool himself that he had done the right thing. No matter how great a lawyer he might have been, or how many people he might have helped, it would not have been worth the lives of two innocent people.

Dimitri is angry and reckless. Ivan is smart and logical. Alyosha is caring and forgiving. And their half-brother Smerdyakov is treated no better than a servant by their father. When Dimitri falls in love with a woman who isn't his fiancée and sets out to get the money his father is keeping from him, tensions within the family run higher than ever.

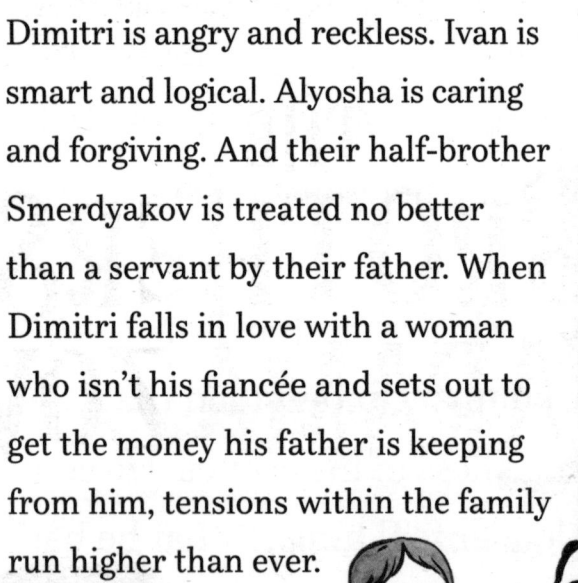

Can Alyosha bring the Karamazov family together before disaster strikes?

Read on for an exclusive sample from the next book in the Easy Classics Epic Collection

THE BROTHERS KARAMAZOV

Fyodor Dostoevsky

Chapter One

Fyodor Karamazov was well known in the pretty town of Skotoprig, but he was not well respected. Despite his large house and vast wealth, he was known to the people of the town as a cruel man.

Fyodor Karamazov loved gambling and money far more than he loved his four sons.

When Fyodor was young, he had captured the heart of a wealthy heiress called Adelaida. Adelaida's family did not approve of Fyodor, sensing that he was not to be trusted. But Adelaida ignored their warnings. They married and had a son called Dimitri.

Fyodor paid little attention to the baby boy, much preferring to spend time gambling with his friends.

When Adelaida died suddenly, Fyodor lost interest in Dimitri altogether.

Adelaida's cousin, Pyotr, could see that Dimitri was being neglected by his father. Pyotr had always been close to Adelaida, so she offered to raise Dimitri herself. Fyodor did not care enough about his son to argue, and so Dimitri was taken away. He grew up in a happy, loving home, only hearing from his father occasionally. Despite his happy upbringing, Dimitri grew up angry with his father. He could not understand why he had been given away.

A few years later, Fyodor married again. Sofya was young and innocent, and had not heard the tales of Fyodor's bad behaviour. She fell deeply in love with him. But despite Sofya's love, Fyodor was still not able to be a good husband. He spent his days at the tavern and disappeared for nights on end.

Sofya had two baby boys. First came Ivan, followed a year later by Alyosha. She loved her boys dearly and protected them when Fyodor returned home in a rage. Eventually, living with Fyodor became too much for Sofya's nerves. She fell gravely ill.

Knowing that she was close to death, Sofya wrote to a friend and begged her to take Ivan and Alyosha to live with her and her husband.

Fyodor's life carried on the way it always had. The only thing he seemed to care about was spending money, which he had inherited from his wives, on lavish parties.

After a few years, Fyodor came to his long-suffering servant, Grigory, with a baby boy. Fyodor told Grigory that the baby was called Smerdyakov and that he needed someone to look after him. Grigory knew that the baby was Fyodor's son, but no one knew who the mother was.

Grigory was a kind man, and extremely loyal to the Karamazov family and his master. With no children of their own, Grigory and his wife gladly accepted the child.

Smerdyakov was the only one of Fyodor's sons to grow up in the Karamazov house.